Walt Disney's

The Old Mill

Margaret Wise Brown

Illustrated by **Philippe Harchy**

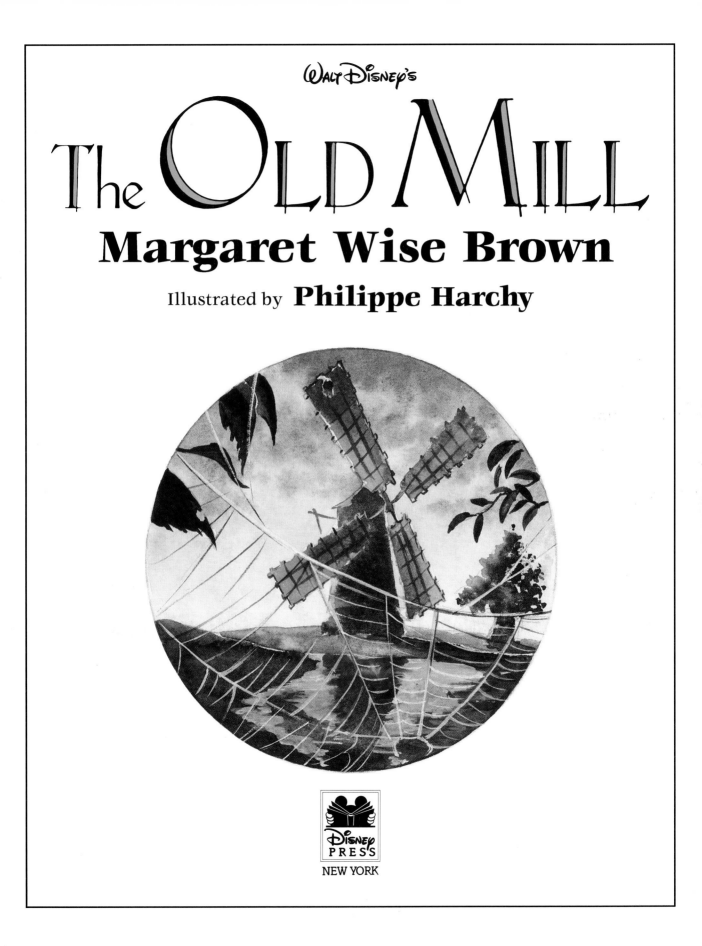

Disney PRESS

NEW YORK

This text originally appeared in the collection entitled *Little Pig's Picnic and Other Stories,*
published by D.C. Heath and Company.
Copyright © 1994 by Disney Press.
All rights reserved.
No part of this book may be used or reproduced
in any manner whatsoever
without written permission from the publisher.
Printed and bound in the United States of America.
For information address Disney Press,
114 Fifth Avenue, New York, New York 10011.
FIRST EDITION
1   3   5   7   9   10   8   6   4   2

Library of Congress Catalog Card Number: 93-74249
ISBN 1-56282-644-1/1-56282-645-X (lib. bdg.)

Walt Disney's The Old Mill

As the sun left the sky, the clouds in the west were gold and gray. The peace of evening came down over the land.

The spider hurried to weave the last strands of his web before dark. The cows went slowly home across the ridge of the hill. And the ducks waddled into the barn.

The windmill stood with its giant ragged arms against the evening sky. Quietness came all around.

The blue barn swallow with the red breast swooped into the old mill. He carried a worm in his beak for his little mate, who was keeping warm their three blue eggs. They were at home in the old mill. Their nest was made in a cog hole of the millstone, for the old mill had not been used for many years except as a home for birds and other animals.

As darkness came on, the old fat owl who slept through the day opened his round yellow eyes. He cocked his head and stamped from one foot to the other. Then he called in a sleepy way, "Whoo! Whoo! Whoo!"

Farther up, bright eyes came out like electric lights in the darkness under the roof. These were the eyes of the bats. The bats lived in the old mill, too, hanging upside down as they slept through the day.

One bat after another unfolded its wings and stretched them wide. They fluttered forth from the old mill like ragged scattered leaves.

Outside, the moon came up in a soft golden mist. The crickets began to chirp in the summer night.

On the pond, as the last of the water lilies closed, two big eyes peered from under a lily pad. Out jumped a big green bullfrog.

He jumped on a lily pad and croaked:
    Come! Come! Come! Come!
And another frog croaked:
    Come where? Come where?
    Come! Come! Come where?
Another frog answered:
    Come here! Come where?
    Come! Come!
And yet another frog croaked:
    Come over there! Come here!
    Come where? Come! Come!
A great chorus of frogs was croaking on the lily pads of the pond. Lightning bugs made hundreds of golden sparks in the darkness.

Then the wind began to blow. It swept through the trees. Great black clouds sailed over the moon. The wind blew harder. Leaves fell down from the trees into the pond, and the frogs dived under the water. Plop!

Then the storm came on in all of its crashing fury.

The old fat owl sitting on a rafter above the mill's waterwheel was nearly thrown from his perch. Water dripped on the fat owl's head and made him angry. He seemed to grow bigger and bigger as he ruffled up his feathers in anger.

Outside, the wind blew the trees low and blew down the fence posts. The slender reeds in the swamp broke off at their lower joints.

Then, in the fury of the storm, the rope that held the mill wheel broke! The arms of the old mill were free once more. They turned round and round against the sky, and the big wheel inside the mill began to turn.

The mother bird on her nest saw the great wheel coming down above her. She fluttered away from the nest in fright. But then she flew back and covered the eggs with her wings. She did not know that the cog for that hole in the millstone was broken. And so the big wheel came rolling over her nest and left her unhurt.

Around and around, the great jagged arms of the windmill turned against the sky. Black clouds went racing over the moon. Lightning flashed in jagged cracks. And inside the mill the great wheel turned around and around over the little mother barn swallow.

The wind shrieked outside, but the little swallow never left her nest. She covered it and kept the eggs warm.

Lightning flashed close by the fat old owl, so he moved sideways on his perch. Then he blinked and turned his head.

The lightning came again with a deafening crash. It struck the old mill and broke off one of the arms of the windmill. The old mill shook, and its turning wheel went more slowly.

The wind died down, and there was only the sound of the rain. And the sound of the rain grew softer and softer until it went away. Then the sky outside grew yellow and light in the east. The moon was gone. And the old mill stood as before. Only now one ragged arm was broken and hanging down against the morning sky.

Inside the mill the old fat owl blinked and closed his eyes. And the bats came flying home.

In the nest under the mill wheel three little birds were opening yellow bills. And the mother and father swallow came flying in. They had worms for their baby birds, who had been born during the storm. The blue feathers of the baby barn swallows were shining in the morning sun.

All was peaceful, as though the storm had never been. The wind and lightning had come and gone. The cows went slowly over the hill. The ducks came out of the barn and swam back to the green reeds by the edge of the pond.

All was quiet as before. The storm had come and gone. And the sunlight was caught in the spider's web.